CARABELLA SNOW

A Whisper In The Wind

Crescent Tales

Written by Pamela Crescent Teel

Illustrated by Anna Johnston

This book is dedicated to the memories of all of my relatives who have since gone on to greener pastures, especially my mom and dad, my grandmothers, Rose, & Crescenza, my Aunt Jo, and all the other caring uncles and aunts that I have had the privilege to know and love.

Remembering you from time to time, remembering with a smile,

How lucky I was to share your life, at least for just a while!

Pam's descriptive manner of writing quickly brings you into the story that she's telling. The environment opens up before your eyes as her characters engage you in their antics, struggles, and humor. Her entertaining stories are a joy to read and a true delight to have on my bookshelf!

-Therese Marchitelli

ABOUT THE ILLUSTRATOR

 Anna Johnston is an artist, primarily painting in oils. Anna received her BFA at the College of New Jersey and resides in Jackson, NJ. She offers private art instruction, in person and on zoom, for all ages, and is certified as a K-12 art teacher. Anna looks forward to creating a new website and expanding her work with Reiki. She is also exploring ways to utilize art to raise awareness, and to help, homeless animals. Anna can be reached by email at annajart2211@gmx.com.

Carabella Snow stood at the edge of the thick enchanted forest, looking out toward the forbidden land known as Castle Cragg. Her blue eyes sparkled brightly, as she wondered what lay beyond the great walls of the stone fortress that sat on top of the distant mountain ridge.

Every now and then, she dared to chase after the sleek team of steeds as they pulled the well-polished carriages through the old forest road, on their way up to the castle. She dreamed, incessantly, of one day hitching a ride on top of one of those carriages and taking a journey that would bring her to a faraway land that she could only imagine.

She also knew that Nollan, king of the Gnomes, and leader of all tiny creatures of the enchanted forest, would punish her severely if she ever acted upon her dreams.

Nollan was the eldest of the Gnomes in the forest. His word had been the law for as long as Carabella could recall. At twilight, the first night of every full moon, Nollan would gather his children around the pulpit, making sure that every one of them was doing their part in caring for the forest. Gaelen, his right-hand gnome, had the task of counting everyone there and calling them to order at the presence of the first full moon.

Nollan would then proceed to take his place behind the podium and give his lecture. Some of what he told the forest creatures was harsh, and sometimes even scary, as the little elves and fairies listened intently to his every word. His lectures, though daunting as they were, were meant to dissuade those curiosity seekers from ever daring to venture beyond the safety of the enchanted forest.

Carabella Snow listened with one ear astray, as Nollan went on and on about the evils of mankind. The more he warned them about these evildoers, the more curious Carabella became of them. Many times, she would spend her whole day at the very edge of the forest, daydreaming.

It was there on the mossy side of the tall pines, lived Aemon. Aemon was a good-natured little elf with long pointy ears, and a mop of dark black hair, which hung loosely over one of his eyes. It was obvious to all that he had a thing for Carabella, though Carabella found him, most of the time, quite annoying.

"Carabella Snow, what are you dreaming about now?" Aemon wondered. He plopped down beside her on the soft velvet moss.

"Nothing that you'd understand," she answered derisively, looking toward the Castle Cragg.

"Actually, I was kind of hoping that you were thinking of me," Aemon replied shyly.

"In your dreams," Carabella scoffed. She fluffed up her wings and hovered above him.

"Come on, Carabella, come back down here," Aemon called out to her, waving his arms high over his head. Carabella chuckled and teased him some more as she flew higher up the tall pine tree. Giggling, she watched as Aemon climbed up after her. He stopped on the branch below.

"I'm not going any higher," he shouted, straddling the branch. He swung his legs back and forth angrily, pretending to ignore her, until she flew down beside him.

"Oh, don't be such a baby, Aemon. I was just playing with you," she told him.

"You know you hurt my feelings when you tease me like that," he replied.

"Then I apologize."

Aemon folded his arms, abruptly. "Nope, not good enough."

"I said I was sorry, what more do you want?" Carabella retorted.

"A kiss would do," he replied, excitedly. Carabella chuckled, as he closed his eyes and pursed his lips together.

"Nice try," she told him, "but it's not going to happen!" She slid off the branch, and into the air she went.

"Hey, where are you going?"

"Home, it's getting late. The moon will be out soon," she yelled down.

"Can't you stay for just a few more minutes?"

"I really should be going, but I will see you tonight at the pulpit. Save me a seat," she called out to him.

Carabella and her friends danced cheerfully around the small campfire waiting for Nollan's grand entrance, but a strange noise soon distracted her. "Did you hear that?" she asked her friends.

"Hear what?" Dana Dewdrop replied.

"Listen."

"What is it that we're listening for?" Lily Frost asked curiously.

"My name, someone was calling out my name. Did you not hear it whispered in the wind?"

"I heard nothing," Petunia Petal told her.

"There it is again," Carabella cried out. "It sounds like it's coming from beyond the enchanted forest."

"And again, we hear nothing," Lily Frost hastily replied.

It wasn't the first time Carabella had heard the voice that carried in the wind, but this one time above all, she felt compelled to find out the source of the whisperer. Luckily, Lily Frost was there to talk her out of it.

"Carabella, save your silly games for another day," Lily cautioned. "The moon is full and anytime now Gaelen will be summoning us to the pulpit." Carabella looked toward the direction of the whispering wind, and then back to her friends. *"Perhaps tonight I shall ask Nollan about the castle and who it might be who calls out my name in the darkness,"* she thought to herself.

The meeting area was already crowded with fairies, trolls, and imps, as Gaelen and Nollan made their way through the crowd and up to the pulpit.

Standing at the podium, pompously, Nollan raised his old knarled cane in the air in a gesture to silence the crowd.

"Children of the natural world, it has come to my attention that over the last few weeks, many strangers have traveled over the old forest road. It deeply concerns me, upon hearing from my trusted trolls, that some of you younger ones even dare to chase the horse-drawn carriages to the very edge of the forest," Nollan stated. He scratched his chin whiskers nervously. "Perhaps even getting close enough to catch a glimpse of what lies within the carriages." Nollan seemed to be looking right at the little fairies, particularly Carabella.

Carabella moved quickly behind Lily Frost, so not to be seen. "Though tempted as you may be, might I remind you that these actions are forbidden. For centuries, we keepers of the forest have lived in harmony among the tall pines and the stilled mountain lakes. As its caretakers, we have taken great measures to remain hidden away from the rest of the world. Why the possibility of even one of us getting caught by the outside world could lead to the gravest of danger for all of us here. Everything that we have strived to protect throughout an eternity would be lost because of the inquisitiveness of the few among us."

Nollan's voice grew louder. He raised his cane higher into the air. "You must take the words that I speak very seriously, for I have told you, repeatedly, that all humans are dangerous, and are not to be trusted! From this day forward, I bequeath that all the creatures of the enchanted forest stay clear of the old forest road until further notice. Take heed, for those who defy my orders shall be banished to the Underworld, forever!"

"The Underworld!" The crowd mumbled fearfully. They gasped at the mere thought of ever being banished to such a cold, dark, damp place, never to return. However, Nollan's warning did nothing to dissuade Carabella from saying what was on her mind.

"How is it that you have come to know that these humans are so dangerous and untrustworthy?" a sole voice rang out through the crowd. Suddenly all fell silent.

"Who is it who dares to ask such a question?" Nollan inquired angrily. The imps pointed over to the fairies, as Petunia Petal gave Carabella a slight nudge forward.

"You, Carabella, of all the fairies here, are the seeker of this question?" Carabella gulped nervously. Nollan looked at her intently. He pondered for a moment before answering.

"Very well, I shall tell you. I have seen with my very own eyes the man who lives beyond the castle walls. He calls himself a king, a ruler among his people, but he is none such. He craves nothing but glory and power as he governs his people with an iron fist. Why, he has an army at his beckon call, and that army has the potential to destroy everyone around him that is kind in nature. Could you imagine the wrath that he would bring down upon us all, Carabella, if he knew that we existed just a stone's throw away from the castle?"

"But he is just one man," Carabella muttered, in a lower voice.

"Did you not listen to a word that I have said, child? Are you not aware of the consequences to those who disobey the laws of this forest?" Nollan stated in a raised voice. "Those who have turned their ears astray have lived to regret it, for they have been long banished to the underworld, never to be seen again. They are resigned to live a dark and lonely existence tending to the twisted roots and the water systems below your very feet, on the ground where you now stand." The crowd looked down at the ground in fear. "I would hate to see that be your fate, Carabella, all because of your curiosity," Nollan scolded. Carabella put her head down in shame.

Her curiosity had bothered Nollan deeply. He had hoped that his words had quelled her, but he knew that the quest for adventure was already in her blood. His thoughts took him back to another time, not so long ago, to another restless fairy who dared to dream about what was beyond the enchanted forest. A faint smile came to his face as he remembered Carabella's mother fondly, but it was soon replaced with one of remorse, for Adelina Snow had vanished years ago, without a trace.

Carabella tried in vain to follow the rules. She stayed away from the old forest road and out of the radar of the mean old trolls, who seemed to make it their business to inform Nollan about everything suspicious. She spent her time resting gently on the soft pine needles of the tallest tree in the forest. It was there that she could see the outline of the castle turret in the distance. It was there that she could dream of the forbidden land that they called Castle Cragg.

Aemon knew where to find her when needed. He called up to her in his high squeaky voice.

"What is it, Aemon?" Carabella shouted down to him. "Why do you always have to bother me?"

"I haven't seen you in a while, Carabella. You haven't come to visit," Aemon answered her. "I was wondering if you were mad at me."

"Now why would I be mad at you? Have you given me any reason to be, except for the fact that you can be a real pain in the neck sometimes," Carabella replied tartly.

"Just because you woke up on the wrong side of the leaf, doesn't mean I have to take it," Aemon retorted. "If you would like me to go, just say so!"

"You're right, I'm sorry, Aemon. I shouldn't take my problems out on you. Please stay?"

"If you really want me too," Aemon answered. He started to climb up the tree. Carabella watched as he climbed higher and higher. Clumsily, he tripped over a vine and nearly lost his footing. Fearful that he would fall, she flew down to meet him.

"Come here and sit, before you fall to your death," she scolded him. "Whatever possessed you to climb so high in the first place?"

Aemon's heart was beating like a drum. "I'd climb to the very top of the tree just for you, Carabella."

"Then you're a fool," she replied. "One strong gust of wind would surely blow you over, and you have no wings to save yourself. Why, you would be a

splat on the ground below," she stated boldly, looking all the way down to the forest floor. "Just settle down and hold on tight."

The two sat together in silence looking out toward the Castle Cragg. They watched as a horse and carriage made their way up the narrow, steep castle road.

"That's a real fancy one," Carabella exclaimed. "Look at those magnificent stallions that pull it."

"Why that carriage shines like liquid gold," Aemon noted. "It must be someone very important!" Carabella stood on her tippy toes and watched the carriage until it was beyond the tree line. She settled back down and sighed.

"What is it, Aemon?" she asked after a few moments of silence.

"I didn't say anything."

"Didn't you just call out my name?"

"No, I did not just call out your name, Carabella."

She put her hand to her ear. "There it is again."

"There what is?"

"My name. Someone is calling out to me."

"But I heard nothing," Aemon replied sincerely.

"As surely as your ears are pointy, Aemon, someone is calling out my name. Though muffled, I can still hear it, like a whisper."

"No reason to get personal here," Aemon retorted, tucking his ears back under his hat. Carabella grabbed him around the waist. "Hold on tight," she told him, then leaped up into the air and spiraled downward until they both landed safely on the soft cedar bed below.

"Thanks," Aemon told her. "I wasn't really looking forward to climbing down." Carabella looked toward the direction of the castle.

"Why Carabella Snow, if I didn't know any better, I'd swear you were up to no good."

"Can you keep a secret, Aemon?"

"It depends on what it is."

"I cannot sleep another restless night tossing and turning with wonder. I am going to find out who it is that whispers my name in the wind. I do feel strongly that the answer lies out there." Carabella pointed toward the Castle Cragg.

"Don't be absurd, Carabella. If Nollan finds out what you're up to, you know that he'll banish you to the Underworld forever. Then I shall never see you again," he stated remorsefully. "Why, you'd be turned into one of those horrible beasts, all white and hunched over; the color of wild roses would be drained from your cheeks, your hair would grow knotty and unkempt," he continued, "and your small delicate hands would become gnarled and as twisted as the underground roots themselves. Are you really willing to take that chance, Carabella, all on just the rumbling of the wind?"

"It's more than just a rumbling, Aemon. It's a feeling in my heart. There's someone out there who desperately needs my help, and I need to find out who it is."

"Very well then, if your mind is made up, then I shall go with you," Aemon replied stoically. "Maybe life in the underworld wouldn't be so bad, with you by my side."

Carabella took his hands in hers. "No, Aemon, this is one journey that I must travel alone. Besides, I need you to stay here and cover for me." Carabella looked around cautiously. "We must speak in private," she whispered. "No telling if the trolls have followed you here. Come with me, Aemon."

Aemon followed her into the thick underbrush. "No one must know what I am about to do," she whispered, "especially the trolls. Should anyone were to ask where I am, I want you to tell them that you were with me just a few minutes ago. Will you do that for me, Aemon?"

"I'll do it for you, but I still don't like the idea of your going all by yourself, Carabella. I should come along to protect you."

"You would do more good right here. Besides, I only need a few hours," Carabella reassured him. "I promise you that I'll be back before the sun goes down."

"You better," Aemon warned her. "I don't know how much longer I could cover for you after that." Carabella took a deep breath as they stepped out of the thickets.

"You'll see, I'll be back before you even miss me," she told him. She gave him a quick kiss on his cheek, fluttered her tiny wings, and off she went. Aemon stayed focused on her until she was just a tiny speck in the sky. Smitten, he touched the cheek that she had kissed. "Hurry back, Carabella," he whispered.

Carabella flew with such speed that it soon tired her out. Spying the castle turret in the distance, she persevered a little further, stopping to rest on a tree branch high up, not far from the castle wall. She shivered, as dark eyes stared out at her from a hollow in the wood. "I'll be on my way now," she muttered, as a big old gray owl let out a loud, forewarning hoot.

The closer Carabella flew to the castle turret, the more distinctly she could hear a faint whimpering. Hovering in the open window, she glanced around before entering. There in the cold sparse room, a young woman lay across her bed, crying into her pillow.

Carabella could hear the loud shuffling of footsteps as they drew closer to the door. She hurried to find a place to hide. Concealing herself behind a dusty book on the shelf, she strained to listen as someone knocked hard on the solid wooden door.

"Wake up, Princess," Calabar, the ailing queen's husband, called out to her. "Make yourself ready, for another suitor will be arriving before noon to claim your hand in matrimony."

"Go away, stepfather," the young princess called out. "I do not want to meet anyone else."

"You have no choice, my dear. I do expect that you will look your best. I will send the maidens up to you in time to help prepare you for your company."

"You can't force me to marry someone I do not love, stepfather," Princess Twila exclaimed.

"Stop your nonsense child, for I have already promised your hand to the highest bidder, in return for all of his riches. And in being that your suitors have been few and far between lately, I have added yet another provision that should bring about a more receptive clientele to claim the hand of the princess. Not

14

only shall the richest suitor have the honor of marrying you, but he will also be appointed as my head knight, leader of all of my soldiers. He will serve me well when I take the throne from your ailing mother. Now make haste, or I shall come back at noon to escort you, myself."

Carabella's heart went out to the princess, as the soft cries of defeat echoed within the walls of the chamber. It wasn't long before the two handmaidens had arrived to help her dress. One of the maidens stroked her hair gently.

"Your stepfather will be well pleased," she spoke out, holding a mirror up for the princess to view herself. "Shall we let him know that you are ready?"

"Give me a moment," the princess replied, dismissing both maidens, and closing the door behind them. Twila made her way over to the window. She leaned over the window ledge as far as she could, looking down at the hard ground sixty feet below. Carabella gasped. She threw the book from the shelf and quickly flew to the princess's side.

"Please, Princess, don't jump," she called out, fluttering her tiny wings in a frenzy.

"Who said that?" Twila wondered, looking around warily.

"It was I," Carabella answered, hovering directly in front of her face.

"Surely, I have been locked up in this turret way too long," the princess muttered.

"Please, I beg of you, come in before you fall to your very death."

"I was only looking for a way to climb down," the princess told her.

"I assure you, there isn't any," Carabella replied.

"My stepfather wants to marry me off to the highest bidder, so he could revel in even more riches. As we speak, another suitor awaits my presence down below. How could I possibly marry someone that I do not love?" Twila exclaimed.

"Perhaps I could help you," Carabella stated. She sighed with relief as the princess came away from the window.

"You truly are real and not just a figment of my imagination?" The princess inquired.

"I am real, Princess."

"I seem to remember, not so long ago, there was another little one, just like you. She also promised to help me, only she never had the chance."

"What do you mean?" Carabella asked. "What happened to her?"

"My stepfather, he somehow found out about her. He set a trap for her."

"Where is she now?"

"I don't know. It's been years since I've last seen her. Calabar kept her hidden somewhere in his bed chamber, and he forbade me to ever speak of her again."

"Tell me, where might I find this chamber?" Carabella asked anxiously.

"I fear to tell you, for I would not want you to meet the same fate as the other little one. Why I don't even know if she is still alive."

"I must see for myself," Carabella stated.

"Calabar would know if his things were disturbed," the princess told her.

"Then I shall be careful not to upset his belongings. I will take a quick look around, and then meet you back here after your suitor has gone," Carabella reasoned.

Twila could hear the footsteps of the maidens coming back for her. "Follow me down the long narrow hallway to the dining hall. I shall pause by his bed chamber and pretend to fix my slipper," she told Carabella. "Please, be careful, you must not let him see you. Surely, he will imprison you too."

The door to Calabar's bed chamber was thick and massive. Carabella tried in vain to push it open. She noticed that there was enough space between the floor and the bottom of the door to squeeze her tiny body through. It was the only way for her to get in.

Brushing off the dust from her wings, she glanced around the room looking for answers. Disappointed at not finding anything out of the ordinary, she started for the door. Just before she was about to shimmy back under, she heard a faint, but steady knocking coming from a large wooden armoire beside the king's massive bed. The armoire door was ajar. Carabella pulled on it with all of her might. She held on tightly as the door slowly swung open a little more, enough where she could fit through. Out of the corner of her eye, she saw something moving from the shadows within. She noticed a clear glass cage, and there, hiding in the corner of the cage, was a tiny little creature, much like herself. Carabella pressed her face to the wall of glass, as the tiny figure slowly lifted up her head.

"Carabella?" the frail fairy cried out.

18

"Mother!" Carabella exclaimed.

"Carabella, my darling daughter, you've come for me. I knew that one day you would hear me calling to you," Adelina cried out, rising feebly from the floor of her cage. Her hand reached out for her daughter's, but the cold glass came between them. Carabella could see how weak and fragile her mother was. Tears streamed down Adelina's white milky cheeks. Carabella shook the cage desperately, trying to free her.

"It's no use, darling, it's locked," Adelina told her, falling back down to her knees. "Listen to me, Carabella; for I am afraid that I have little time left in this world. With each passing day, my powers have grown weaker and weaker. Though it comforts me to see your lovely face one last time, I bid you to go. Leave now, my darling, and never look back."

"No mother, please, you must hold on for just a little while longer. I will find a way to free you, I promise," Carabella cried out.

The sound of trumpets blaring in the background startled Carabella. "I must go now, but I will be back for you mother, if it's the last thing that I do," she vowed.

"My precious little girl, stay far away from Calabar," her mother warned her. "If he catches you, he will drain the spark of life from your body, as he has done to me."

"I have no intention of getting caught by him, mother," Carabella reassured her. "Just promise me that you'll hold on while I go and get help."

19

"I will try," Adelina told her. Carabella blew her mother a kiss and then slowly closed the chest door.

The princess was still in the dining hall. Carabella entered and hid from view. She noticed a short stocky bald-headed man bending over, trying to kiss the princess's hand. In disgust, Twila quickly withdrew her hand from his hold. The suitor stood there awkwardly, smiling up at her. Two footmen, carrying trunks, lay them down at Calabar's feet.

"I have traveled a great distance to bring you my treasures, Sire, and I look forward, with great anticipation, to claiming both of my prizes," Alabash commented, glancing over at the princess. He reached down and opened the first chest. "I bring you treasures from my homeland, Princess." Calabar's eyes dimmed as Alabash pulled out a handful of linens. "I bring you the finest materials, handmade by the craftiest women in my village. Perhaps even a wedding dress can be sown from such fine textile," Alabash hinted. Calabar frowned with discontent. "Does this not please you?" Alabash asked him.

"They certainly are of fine substance, but not exactly what I had in mind. Surely, a mere morsel of what the princess is truly worth," Calabar argued.

"Then, perhaps this would please you more," Alabash exclaimed, pulling out a small purple pouch from under his shirt. He opened it slowly and proceeded to pour a few golden nuggets onto the table.

"Ah, now this is more like it!" Calabar exclaimed. His eyes lit up like two full moons. "Pray tell, how many more have you in there?"

"Enough to buy two princesses, Sire," Alabash jested. Calabar looked the nuggets over diligently.

"As you can see, the nuggets, they are of real gold," Alabash noted.

Calabar seemed delighted. "Yes, they certainly feel real." With little deliberation, he accepted the gifts. "No doubt, you are the richest contender thus far," he stated, "but there are still three nights left before the contest ends. I must honor my words to that midnight hour. In the meantime, you shall stay and be a guest here at my castle." Alabash happily accepted. "You must dine with us tonight. I will tell the servants to set an extra plate at the table."

"I shall be honored to dine with both you and the princess tonight." Alabash then addressed the princess. "Perhaps we can get to know each other better, my dear."

"I shall not be very hungry tonight," Twila replied, repulsed by the very thought of it. Calabar gave his stepdaughter a warning glance.

"She will be at dinner," Calabar promised. "In the meantime, I think we should lock these jewels away for safekeeping."

"Yes," Alabash agreed, handing the purple pouch over to Calabar. "We must keep them safe." Alabash, once again, tried to take the princess's hand, but ended up tripping over his own two feet, landing face down in front of Twila. The princess couldn't help but let out a soft chuckle before she excused herself. The maidens accompanied her back up to her room, and by Calabar's orders, locked the door behind them.

Throwing off her gown, Twila slipped into a simpler dress, then fell onto her bed in dismay. "Don't fret Princess, there are still three more days before you're doomed to marry that frog," Carabella told her. "I will do what I can to help you." The princess looked up at her. "At least I stopped him from slobbering all over your hand."

"That was you who tripped him?"

"And I will do it again, and again, if need be," Carabella replied.

"Tell me, did you find what you were looking for in Calabar's chamber?"

"Yes, Princess, I found much more than I had expected to. For you see, it is my mother for whom your stepfather has imprisoned in his cage of glass."

"Your mother?" The princess was stunned at the revelation. "Then I know how you must have longed for her, after all these years apart, for my mother has also been imprisoned by Calabar. He has locked her far away from me, on the other side of the castle. I have been informed by my maidens that she is very ill. Calabar swears that they are doing everything that they can for her, but I don't believe him, not for one moment. I don't even want to think about the power that he will one day wield if my mother should perish."

"Then together, we shall find a way to free both your mother and mine, as well," Carabella told her.

"But how do we fight a man like Calabar? He never seems to lose," the princess cried out.

Carabella wasn't quite sure how to answer her, but she knew that she couldn't sit back and do nothing. She wrestled the whole way home with the thought of asking Nollan for help, but she couldn't risk the consequences of being banished to the Underworld, forever. Still, she would have traded her life in a heartbeat, if it meant freedom for her mother and the princess's mother.

Carabella darted skillfully between the tall pines, looking out below for the spying trolls, and Aemon.

"There you are," she panted, nearly out of breath. She landed beside him. "I've been searching everywhere for you?" Aemon looked worried. "Is everything all right?" she asked.

"No, everything is not all right," Aemon stated nervously. "Everything has gone awry since you've been gone."

"What do you mean, Aemon? Did someone find out where I went?"

"No, it's not always about you, Carabella."

"That's good," she answered with a sigh of relief. "Then what is it?"

Aemon looked around suspiciously. "Come with me," he whispered. "There's something, or rather, someone, I need to show you."

"Can it wait? There's something really important that I need to talk to you about first."

"No, I'm afraid it can't wait," Aemon insisted. Reluctantly, Carabella followed him deep into the woods.

"Why do you keep looking back over our shoulder?" Carabella asked him curiously.

"Because I want to be sure that the trolls aren't following us."

"Why?"

"You will see soon enough, Carabella. Quickly, over here," he directed her. He began to pull up broken tree branches from the ground, exposing a long figure lying in the soft grass.

"What is it, Aemon?" Carabella asked inquisitively.

"It's one of them. I found him lying by the old forest road. He was hurt and bleeding. I couldn't just leave him there."

"Is he conscious?"

"He's been in and out of consciousness for some time now."

"Look, his shoulder is bleeding," Carabella exclaimed.

"How'd I miss that one?" Aemon wondered, tearing off another piece of his shirt. "Any more wounds and I won't have a shirt left," he quipped. He soaked the torn shirt in the nearby pond, and then placed it over the wound. Suddenly, his eyes began to flutter open.

"Quickly, we must disappear," Carabella warned Aemon.

"Too late for that, he's already seen me, although he might think that he was dreaming, or delirious."

"Does anyone else know that he's here?" Carabella whispered.

"I don't think so. I was crossing the old forest road at the time, and you know quite well that we were forbidden to be anywhere around there. I made myself invisible so the trolls wouldn't see me. It looked like he had been badly beaten and then dumped into the high grass. He had a nasty wound on his side." Aemon felt the young man's forehead. "I fear his fever has gotten worse, Carabella. He will surely die if we don't help him."

25

"Then I shall go and gather some herbs from the forest to help bring down his fever. You wait here with him, Aemon. I'll be right back."

"Carabella, be careful not to draw any attention to yourself," Aemon reminded her.

When Carabella returned, she placed some wet leaves over the young man's wounds. He winced with pain. "Hey, what are you doing?" he inquired.

"We're trying to help you. Lie still so your wounds can heal properly," Carabella told him.

The young stranger looked around feverishly. "Where am I?"

"You're in the enchanted forest," she replied. She couldn't help but notice how handsome the young man was. His straight brown hair fell to one side, and his eyes were as green as the forest pines. Carabella could see that he was very anxious. "Don't worry, you're among friends here," she reassured him. The young stranger tried to sit up.

"Can you tell me how far away I am from Castle Cragg?"

"You're just a stone's throw," Aemon replied.

"Is that where you were heading before you had your accident?" Carabella inquired.

"Yes, that was my plan."

"So, you were going to claim the hand of the princess?" Carabella inquired.

"Princess, I know nothing about a princess," the young man stated. "I was on my way to the castle to strike a deal with a man called Calabar, when I was suddenly ambushed by a den of thieves. They took my horse and all of the gold that I carried in my pouch."

"Then you know nothing of the contest?" Carabella asked.

"What contest would that be?" the young man inquired.

"Calabar has promised his stepdaughter's hand in marriage to the suitor who brings the richest in treasure to him, before the midnight hour, three days from now."

"I know nothing of such a contest, nor do I care to marry a princess," the young man reiterated. "I merely wished to speak to Calabar about a subject matter that is dear to my heart. In exchange for his cooperation, I was to offer him my pouch of gold. Now I fear that he will not listen to me."

"You are right about that," Carabella went on. "Calabar will not listen to you, not without your gold. Though he is not yet officially the King, he does command his army with a fierce hand. You would be wise to avoid him, for he is not to be trusted. He keeps the rightful heir to the throne and her daughter locked away in separate chambers, under watchful eyes."

"How do you know this?" The young man asked.

"Because I have recently been to the castle, and I have spoken with the princess herself. I have seen the evil, firsthand, that Calabar has brought forth, and I believe I have also seen your gold."

"How do you know that it was my gold?"

28

"Tell me this, what was the color of the pouch that you carried your gold in?"

"It was purple."

"And the man who robbed you, was he tall and thin?"

"No, he was short, fat, and balding. I fought them off, but one of his footmen pierced my side with his dagger, then knocked me on the side of my head. They stole my pouch from me."

"You are correct about the man. He was short and balding, and the pouch he presented to Calabar was indeed purple," Carabella told him.

"Then it was my gold."

"The bald one, the one who looks like a fat old bullfrog, he goes by the name of Alabash. He is a guest at the castle, as we speak," Carabella told him.

The young man tried to stand up. "I must go and retrieve what he took from me."

"No, you must take this day to rest up and let the herbs heal you," Carabella told him. "You will be no good in your condition confronting his footmen. You need to rest now. Later when you wake, we shall devise a plan together to get you into the castle. Aemon and I will help you get your gold back, but in return, you must do something for us."

"What is it that you ask of me?"

"You must help me save the lives of the princess, her mother, and another."

"I shall offer you my services in any way that I can," the young man vowed. "I suddenly feel faint." He rested his head back down on the soft pine needles.

"That means the herbs are working. I gave you something to help you rest," Carabella replied. "Sleep now, tall stranger, gather your strength, for our journey is yet to come."

"Rogan, my name is Rogan," the young man muttered, just before closing his eyes. Aemon covered him back up with branches and twigs, unaware that Lily Frost was watching from above.

Aemon and Carabella waited impatiently for the nighttime to come. When it did, they went to check on Rogan.

"Did you sleep well, young Rogan?" Aemon inquired.

"Yes, better than expected. Thank you for the tea you brought earlier. I was quite parched."

Carabella looked puzzled. "Tea, we didn't bring you any tea. Perhaps you were dreaming?"

"Perhaps, but I could have sworn that I drank tea earlier. Did you not sit next to me as I drank?"

"I did not. We waited until the darkness to return," Carabella told him.

"Then perhaps, I was dreaming," Rogan reasoned. "I'd like to thank the two of you for what you have done for me."

"It was Aemon who found you and brought you here. He deserves the thanks," Carabella replied.

"It must have been tough for a little guy like yourself to drag my lifeless body deep into the forest," Rogan stated.

Aemon put his hands on his hips. "I'm not that little," he quipped.

"You're right, you're not." Rogan stood corrected. "You're actually very brave for a...

"Elf," Aemon answered.

"Don't be silly, there's no such thing as elves," Rogan chuckled.

"I suppose there are no such things as fairies either," Carabella chimed in, kicking up her heels, and twirling in the air just above him.

"You two do seem very real to me," Rogan reasoned. "No, it must have been that bump on the head, or those herbs that you gave me."

Carabella turned to Aemon. "Come to think of it, how did you carry young Rogan all the way here?"

"It was easy. I just lifted him and dragged him through the woods. He wasn't really that heavy," Aemon replied, unaware that it was really the hands of the creatures of the underworld that did most of the lifting.

Rogan rose suddenly to his feet. "I need to stand up and move around if I'm ever going to retrieve my gold, and save a princess." He leaned against the tree for support.

"You're still very weak, young Rogan," Carabella observed. "You need more time for healing. I will go and gather some more herbs for you."

"I'll be fine," Rogan replied, unconvincingly. "I feel strong enough to fight." He took one step forward before falling back onto his knees.

"Perhaps tomorrow," Aemon reasoned with him. Rogan looked around for his belongings. "Where is my sword? I must find my sword."

"It must be in the underbrush where I found you. I will go and search for it while you stay here and rest," Aemon told him.

Deep into the woods, Rogan rested, where no one could find him. When he woke, he found a leather satchel filled with cold water by his side, and a large leaf-covered with fruits and berries for him to eat. He smiled gratefully, then quickly swallowed a handful of wild blueberries. They felt good going down, for his stomach had been empty with hunger.

Rogan noticed a shiny object leaning against one of the trees. Slowly, he made his way over to it. It wasn't his sword, but he picked it up anyway and examined it. It was long and weighty, and definitely twice as nice as the one he had. He sliced the air a few times with it. Worn out, he lay the sword down by his side.

That night, Rogan looked up at the half moon and prayed. He bowed his head obediently. "Oh, great glory of the heavens, I am nothing but a mere herder of sheep, but tomorrow I must free a princess and retrieve that which was stolen from me," he called out. "The people of my village have entrusted me with all of their worth so that I may speak to Calabar on their behalf. I ask that you give me the strength and the courage to carry out such a great task." Rogan paused briefly. "There is one more thing that I do ask of you, I ask that you bless these little creatures of the forest, and that you watch over them and protect them, for I will be eternally indebted to them. Please keep them safe and out of harm's way, forever." Rogan thought he heard a slight whimper. He looked around quickly.

"Is someone there?" he called out, but no one answered.

By morning, Rogan felt fresh and alert, wanting nothing more than to explore his surroundings. Carabella had warned him not to wander too far from his place of hiding. For the time, he could do nothing but wait for the two to come back.

"How are you feeling today, young Rogan?" Carabella inquired.

"I feel strong, and rested, and ready to slay the dragon," he replied confidently. He secured his new sword in his sash.

"Actually, you don't need to worry about the dragon anymore," Aemon told him. "We took care of him a very long time ago."

"How are your wounds today?" Carabella inquired.

"They're healing just fine, thank you," Rogan answered, lifting his shirt up for them to see. Carabella blushed slightly at the sight of his naked chest. "Those extra herbs that you brought for me last night have surely done their job."

"But I didn't bring you any extra herbs last night," Carabella replied.

"I see you found your sword," Aemon interrupted. "Where did you find it? I looked everywhere."

"Actually, it's not my sword. This sword sort of found me," Rogan told them both. "Though I feel compelled to tell you, no sword in my possession has ever seen another man's blood."

"Then why do you carry one?" Aemon inquired.

"I find it valuable for cutting down the thicket when my sheep wander too far into the bush," Rogan answered truthfully. Rogan felt strong enough to wash himself in the nearby stream. He slicked his hair back and tightened his sash to further secure his new sword.

Carabella turned to the skies above. "The sun shall soon be full upon us, young Rogan. We must leave now for the castle."

"No Carabella, you must stay here. Aemon has told me of the trouble that will befall you if you dare to leave the forest again. I could not stand it if you were punished for coming to my aid," Rogan told her. "I don't want you to worry, for I will honor my debt to you, and free the princess, and your mother too. For this, you have my word."

"Aemon told you about my mother?"

"Yes, he told me everything. You have a good friend in him, Carabella. I will do my very best to free both the princess and your mother. Wait for me by the forest edge, if you must, but go no further."

Carabella and Aemon kept visual all morning in the tall pine tree at the edge of the forest, unaware that they weren't the only ones keeping an eye out for young Rogan.

"He should be there by now, don't you think?" Carabella inquired.

"I suppose so," Aemon answered.

"I should have gone with him. I was the one who promised the princess and my mother that I would be back for them," she stated.

"Give him a chance, Carabella. It is still early." Aemon tried to reassure her.

Rogan knocked on the massive door before him.

Feeling a little intimidated by its size, he knocked louder. He waited impatiently as the door slowly opened. A servant blocked the entrance.

"What is it you want here?" the servant asked curiously.

"I want to see Calabar."

"That is Sir Calabar to you. Soon to be king of all this land," the servant bellowed.

"Very well, then I want to see Sir Calabar," Rogan replied, rather sarcastically.

"State your business," the servant demanded.

"I've come about my gold."

"Where are your trunks?"

"I have only what you see," Rogan told him.

"Then Sir Calabar will not be interested in seeing you. Leave now, bring your business elsewhere." Rogan held the door open with his foot.

"But the king already has my gold," he argued. "It arrived earlier."

"Why didn't you say so?" the servant retorted. "I take it that you are a suitor for the princess?"

"I guess so," Rogan answered. "If that's what it takes to get me in," he mumbled under his breath. The servant stood aside, as Rogan quickly brushed past him. "Now where may I find Calabar?"

"He is in his chambers. It is still early, and Sir Calabar is not an early riser. You may go into the kitchen and have some fresh bread and tea while you wait." The servant pointed across the massive hallway. "I will come for you when the time is right."

"Thank you, that is most kind and generous of you," Rogan replied. He walked slowly across the gray-stoned entranceway. He waited for the servant to leave, then took the opportunity to look around the castle for himself. Cautiously, he climbed up the steep, winding staircase before him. In front of him was a long hallway. Directly ahead of him was a single door. He tiptoed up to the door and put his ear against it. Clearly, he could hear whimpering from within. He tried the door handle, but the door was locked. It made him sad to hear that someone was sobbing.

"Who is it that cries behind this locked chamber door," Rogan whispered into the keyhole. Princess Twila lifted her head from her pillow and looked around the room.

"Is someone there?" she called out. She quickly raced over to the door. She tried to open it, but it was still locked.

"Is that you, Princess?"

"Who is it who inquires?"

"I am but your humble servant sent here by a mutual friend to help you."

"And what name does this mutual friend go by?" the princess asked curiously.

"Her name is Carabella."

"Carabella!" The princess recollected the little fairy with delight. "She did make me a promise that she would find a way to help me."

"And that would be me," Rogan replied, rather sure of himself. "Fear not Princess, for I shall free you, but first I must speak with Calabar."

"Calabar?" the princess cried out. "He will not listen to you on such matters of my freedom; not unless you've brought riches greater than Alabash."

"Alabash, the thief!" Rogan exclaimed.

"That thief, I fear, will be my husband in less than forty-eight hours," Twila cried out.

"Then I must work fast to stop that from happening. I will take my leave for now, but I will be back."

"Friend of Carabella's, you must listen to me, you must stay away from my stepfather, for he will not listen to your reasoning." Twila tried to warn him, but Rogan had already taken to the stairs.

Rogan waited in the kitchen by the warm ovens for the servant to come back for him. "Another slice of bread?" Sala, the kitchen maiden, asked him.

"No thank you, the first one was quite filling. Please, fair maiden, would you tell me of the princess?"

"What is it you wish to know?" Sala inquired.

"Why is she locked in her bed chamber, and why is Calabar trying to marry her off to someone she clearly does not want to be with?"

"You ask many questions for a young suitor; questions that shouldn't concern you," Sala replied. She couldn't help but notice how handsome the young man was. In some small way, he reminded her of someone else, but she couldn't remember who. His only fault was in being young and naive.

"Can you keep a secret?" Rogan whispered. Sala gave him a nod. "I've come to free the princess from her bondage."

"Then you have brought a pot of gold?" Sala jested.

"A pot of gold? I'm afraid not," Rogan replied.

"Then how do you, a mere boy yourself, intend on pulling off such a feat?"

"I'm waiting to speak with Calabar."

"You wish to speak to Calabar about freeing his stepdaughter? Have you no fear for your life, child?"

"I am not afraid of that I do not know," Rogan told her.

"Then know this, Calabar will make minced pie of you if you don't have a substantial offering for him. Young man, run from this castle while you still can. Come, I will show you the back way out."

"I am not going anywhere until I speak to Calabar," Rogan insisted.

"Don't say that I didn't warn you," Sala replied. She took the ball of dough that she was kneading and brought it to another table. Rogan followed close behind.

"You never did tell me about the princess. What is she like?" Sala looked up at him impatiently, but she knew he wasn't going to back down so easily.

"Princess Twila," Sala went on, "why she's a vision of beauty. She's a mere child though, much like yourself. The more she matures, the more she looks like her mother, our queen. Both women have hearts filled with nothing but goodness." Rogan waited while Sala placed the dough into the oven.

"Please, do continue. What color is her hair?"

"Her hair is spun of yellow gold, and her eyes as blue as an aquamarine gemstone," Sala answered. "Surely, have you not seen her for yourself?"

"I have never laid eyes upon her, but I have heard the sadness in her voice through the locked door of her bed chamber."

"You were at her chamber door?"

"Yes, and all I can say of her is that her voice is as sweet as the melody of the birds in the meadows. I have vowed to free both her, and her ailing mother, and I intend to make good on my promises," Rogan replied.

"Not even a magician could save the queen now, for she is heavily guarded by Sir Calabar's men. Even I, once the queen's personal handmaiden, have not seen her for weeks now. Sadly, I fear the worse. You are a young fool if you think you alone can take on Calabar and his army of blackhearts. Many have tried before you, and all have failed. You can count their scattered bones for yourself down in the mountain's crevice behind the castle walls, exposed for all to see," Sala told him. "You must leave while you can young man before you end up like the others."

"I will speak with Calabar first," Rogan retorted. He turned toward the doorway. "Well, it's about time," he muttered, as the servant finally came back for him. Rogan followed him across the stone floor and into another hallway of the castle.

"Sir Calabar is waiting for you in there," the servant told him. Rogan walked into the large room. There in front of him, sitting comfortably on his high-backed red velvet chair, next to a roaring fire, sat Calabar.

"You may step forward," the servant directed him.

"Ah, so you've come to claim Princess Twila's hand?" Calabar inquired.

"I have come to speak with you about many things," Rogan began, "but first I would like to discuss the issue of my gold."

"Gold, you've brought me gold?"

"In truth, sir, you already are in possession of my gold. My purple satchel has already been presented to you, by the hands of a thief who calls himself Alabash."

"You say that your gold was stolen from you?" Calabar inquired.

"That is a fact, sir, stolen by the very man who is a guest here in your castle."

"Tell me, how did this come to be?" Calabar asked, bewildered.

"A few nights back, while on my way to the castle, I was ambushed by Alabash and his two footmen," Rogan went on. "I was injured and left for dead by the side of the old forest road."

"What a tall tale you weave, young stranger," Calabar chuckled.

"I assure you, sir, it is no tale." Calabar quickly called his servant to his side and whispered something into his ear. Within seconds, the servant was gone from the room. "My servant has gone to fetch Alabash and bring him here. We shall see what he has to say about such accusations."

Rogan waited impatiently for Alabash to enter the room. "That's him, that's the thief," he called out. "You are the one who stole my gold, and my horse too." Rogan lunged toward him. One of Calabar's guards came between them.

"Alabash, is this true?" Calabar asked him.

"I assure you, Sire, I do not know what this boy is talking about? Why, I've never seen him before in my life."

41

"This young man accuses you of robbing him and taking his gold. You say that this is not the truth?"

"Sire, the gold that I have presented to you was my very own," Alabash stated innocently.

"You are a liar," Rogan cried out.

"Surely, sire, I am not the one who lies," Alabash retorted.

"I was resting my horse by the side of the road when out of nowhere his two footmen came upon me. One of them wounded me with his dagger while the other held me down. They cut my pouch from my sash, hit me on the head, and threw me into the tall grass," Rogan exclaimed. "That gold was to be given to you in exchange for a promise."

"And what promise would that be?" Calabar inquired curiously.

"The promise that the people of my village would be spared from the ravage of your soldiers as they constantly pillage our small, but humble abode. They come and they feast on our stored meats and vegetables until our people have nothing left to feed their very own children. Our soil is rocky. We have a hard time as it is growing enough crops to get us all through the winter. I fear our food supply will be scarce this coming season because of your soldiers," Rogan went on. "Seeing that you already have my satchel of gold, I ask for your word to help resolve the matter of your derelict army."

"But you have yet to prove that the gold is truly yours?" Calabar replied.

"You have my word that the gold is mine!" Rogan exclaimed.

"The word of a child," Alabash interrupted. "Surely, sire, anyone can see that the boy is lying. I carried that gold all the way from my homeland along with my trunks of fine linen. Ask my two footmen, and they will tell you the same. That is why I brought them along with me, to see that my gold was delivered safely to you."

"You are the only liar here, Alabash, you and your henchmen who stole that gold from me," Rogan shouted. "Wait, I can prove that I was attacked. One of Alabash's men pierced my side with his dagger. I still have the wound. See for yourself." Rogan lifted up his shirt, exposing his bare skin. "Now do you believe me?"

Calabar looked intently at Rogan's side. "What kind of a game are you playing here, boy?" he stated angrily. "I see no such wound."

"It's right here," Rogan pointed. He looked down at his side. His skin was smooth and free of any wound. "It was here just yesterday," he muttered.

Alabash chuckled loudly. "So, now you are telling us that your wound disappeared, just like that. Surely, sire, you can see that the boy is not all there," he stated, pointing to his head.

"My horse, you took my horse from me. Where is he? That would be proof enough that there was indeed foul play," Rogan shot back.

"Once again I am accused of something that I did not do," Alabash argued. "I do not have this young fool's horse, nor his gold, sire."

"You're a liar, Alabash. Give me back my gold," Rogan demanded.

"I understand your desperation in wanting to help your people," Alabash sympathized, "but I am not willing to give up my gold for you to do so. Surely, sire, you can see that the boy came here with nothing to barter with. Why he has concocted this whole story in order to rob me of my riches. I will not let him make a mockery of me any longer. I will take my gold and leave."

"That will not be necessary, Alabash. I have heard quite enough. With the gold that you have brought, it is you who shall marry Princess Twila and claim your seat as head knight two days from now."

"The princess will not marry the likes of you, Alabash," Rogan shouted.

"What the princess truly wants is of no concern of yours," Calabar retorted. "It shall be as it is, the day after tomorrow; if no other suitors come forward bearing greater gifts, then Alabash, you shall claim what is yours." Calabar turned to Rogan. "Since you have not proven this gold to be yours, I have nothing further to discuss with you."

"What about the people of my village?" Rogan inquired.

"I can not help you. Come back when you have something to barter with, and then perhaps, I shall listen," Calabar stated bitterly.

"I will not leave without a fight," Rogan shouted. He grabbed hold of Alabash's arm and twirled him around. Alabash let out a loud howling moan.

"How dare you injure a guest of my castle?" Calabar called out. "Apologize to him, now!" he demanded.

"I will do no such thing," Rogan countered.

"Clearly this boy needs to learn a lesson," Calabar quipped. "Guards, take him and throw him in the dungeon. Let him rot there for a few days while I decide what to do with him."

"Let go of me," Rogan shouted. It took two of Calabar's men to drag him out of the room. "I will get you, Alabash. I will make you pay for what you have done." Alabash grinned devilishly. Sala looked at Rogan, sympathetically, as they went by. The princess paced back and forth in her room waiting for news of her mystery man. She sighed with disappointment as Sala unlocked her door and brought her dinner tray in. She lay the tray down on the table and turned to leave. "Please, don't go yet."

"Very well, Princess."

"Sala, my friend, tell me, has there been a stranger at the castle today other than that oath, Alabash?"

Sala hesitated to answer. "There was a young man who came by this morning," she confessed. "It seems he was on a mission. He wanted to speak with your stepfather."

"What kind of a mission?"

"He came to speak on behalf of the people of his village. He also claimed that Alabash had stolen his gold. The very gold that he came here to barter with for the safety of the people in his village."

"If this is true and the gold is really his, then I would not have to marry Alabash after all!" the princess exclaimed.

"I, for one believe it to be true, for when I looked into the young man's noble face, I saw nothing but honesty," Sala told her. "I'm afraid your stepfather thought otherwise. Young Rogan had failed to prove that the gold was his, and Alabash denied all of his accusations."

"Did this young Rogan say anything else?" the princess wondered.

"When I spoke with him earlier in the kitchen, he had this wild notion in his head that he was going free both you and your mother."

"Then it was he who came to my chamber door this morning," Twila reasoned.

"He caused quite a stir. I warned him not to go up against Calabar," Sala fretted.

"Where is he now?" Twila asked. "Did my stepfather send him away?"

"I'm afraid to say, he's been taken to the dungeon."

"The dungeon?" Twila suddenly felt ill. "Sala, we must free him. You know what will happen to him if we don't."

"Yes, sadly he'll end up a pile of bones behind the castle walls," Sala noted.

"Then you'll help me?"

"I'll not have anything to do with it," Sala replied sternly.

"Please Sala, I beg of you."

"And what of me? If I get caught, I shall no doubt join him yonder in the boneyard," Sala argued.

"Then I, alone, shall set him free. Leave my door unlocked when you go. I will give you a fair amount of time to be clear of this before I sneak down to the dungeon," Twila pleaded. Sala thought for a moment.

"Very well, I shall leave the door unlocked. That is all I can do," she replied hastily.

"That is all I ask from you." Twila waited a few minutes to give Sala time to go back down before sneaking out into the hallway. She tiptoed lightly down the long winding stairwell and quietly made her way to the dungeon.

She couldn't help but gag as she entered the cold dank prison. Holding her hand over her nose, she searched the cells. A chill ran down her spine as a lone skeleton, still shackled at the wrists, hung from one of the walls. Twila heard something moving before her. Frightened, she stepped back into the shadows.

"Please, don't be afraid. I'm in no position to hurt you," someone called over to her.

"You were the one at my bedroom door this morning?" Twila asked nervously.

"Yes, and you must be the princess," Rogan answered. Twila stepped from the shadows into the dim light.She couldn't help but smile, as their eyes met for the very first time.

"It's a pleasure to meet you, Princess. Sorry, I don't have better news for you," Rogan apologized.

"Quickly, I must free you before anyone knows that I am gone from my room."

"The keys are up there on that shelf," Rogan told her. "I saw one of the guards put them there." The shelf was higher than Twila. Rogan watched as she dragged a stool over and climbed up on it. "Careful Princess, I would not want you to hurt yourself." Twila found the keys and then jumped down from the stool.

"We must hurry before the guards come back," she told him. She fumbled to find the right key. Relieved when she heard the lock unclick, she stood back as Rogan pushed open the heavy metal door.

"You must leave here at once," Twila stated. "Come with me and I will show you the way out."

Rogan retrieved his sword from the ground and followed Twila up the stairs and into a small alcove that led to the kitchen. Sala stood waiting. "This way quickly, or it'll be my head," she told them, opening a small servant door that led out to the woods behind the castle.

"Go Rogan, and don't stop until you are far away from this place," Twila warned him. "You are never to come back here, do you understand?" Rogan hesitated to leave.

"Hurry, please, someone is approaching," Sala whispered. The princess and Sala hid behind the stone wall. Rogan tried to hide, but it was too late. One of Calabar's men spotted him and came running. Thinking quickly, Sala stuck her foot out from the shadows just as the guard ran past her. He lost his balance and hit the solid rock wall with such force that it knocked him out.

"Oops," Sala remarked. "Papa always said that I had big feet." Twila grabbed hold of Rogan's hand.

"Go now, before it's too late."

"Not without you, Princess," Rogan replied, gripping her hand tightly.

"But my mother…"

"I'll come back for her, I promise you, but first I need to get you to safety."

"Young Rogan is right; you should go with him, unless you want to end up marrying Alabash in two days' time," Sala reasoned. "Go now, the two of you, before the guard wakes." Sala held the narrow door open as the two went through. Twila turned to give Sala a quick hug. "Get as far away from here as you can, for your own safety, Princess."

"Hurry," Rogan told her. "We have to leave now. We need to take advantage of this head start if we're going to make it across the open meadow."

"Where will you take me, brave Rogan?"

"To the forest. I have friends there. They will keep us safe," he assured her.

He knew that there would be a good chance of being seen from the watchtower if they crossed the open meadow and that Calabar's soldiers would be upon them with their horses before they reached the forest. "We must take a different way to the forest," Rogan told her. "It'll be longer, but we need to stay hidden as long as we can." He led the princess down into a steep ravine that eventually led to the river. "Walk on the rocks whenever you can. They'll be fewer tracks for the guards to follow." Rogan held his hand out to steady her. "I'm sorry, I know this is hard for you."

"I've been to this river many times before, brave Rogan. When my real father was alive, we would walk for hours down here in this very ravine. So much has changed since then, but how is it that you know this trail to the forest?"

"I don't quite remember, but I think I've been here before," Rogan answered honestly. "Up ahead should be the open meadow, but we will be further away from the castle, and it will be less too cross in the open. Hopefully they will not see us."

"How I worry about my mother being up there all alone," the princess cried out.

"Don't worry about your mother, Princess. When you are safe from any harm, I will find a way to go back and free her," Rogan promised. Rogan led her through the shallow water, and then toward the meadow.

"How do you know we'll be safe where we're going?" the princess asked him.

"Because my friends will keep you safe and well hidden. Trust me, Princess," Rogan smiled, "but for now we must keep on moving."

"I must insist, brave Rogan, that you call me by my birth name, Twila. Besides, I don't feel much like a princess right now."

Rogan turned and looked at her. "Very well, Twila." Twila could feel her cheeks redden as she stared into his young handsome face. Feeling a bit flushed himself; Rogan couldn't help but smile back at her. He was relieved to see that there were no signs of Calabar's men behind them as they approached the area of the meadow that they still had to cross. "We are much further down, and hopefully out of view of the watch guards, but we still must cross the meadow here to get to the forest. We cannot stop running, Twila, not until we reach the other side. Are you ready?"

Twila nodded that she was ready. Rogan took hold of her hand and they started to run. He could see the forest getting closer and closer. He felt confident that they were going to make it.

"Rogan," Twila suddenly called out in horror, "the soldiers, they are upon us." Rogan turned to see three men on horseback riding swiftly towards them.

"Run faster, we're almost there," he shouted, as they raced through the tall fescue. It was futile as the tall grass seemed to slow them down. One of the soldier's horses galloped ahead and intercepted them. The other two men took up the flank, surrounding them. Rogan took his sword from his sash and stood in front of the princess.

"You silly child," one of Calabar's guards called out to him. He quickly dismounted from his horse. Rogan raised his sword high in the air.

"Looks like the boy wishes to fight," another of the guards commented.

"Come no further," Rogan declared, holding the sword out before him.

"Step aside, you young fool. We come for the princess."

"I will not let you take her back," Rogan threatened, shielding Twila with his own body.

"Very well," the guard stated, then drew his sword. "If it's a fight you want, I'll be happy to oblige."

"Young Rogan's in trouble," Carabella called out from the tall pine tree at the edge of the forest. "I have to help him." She flew down to Aemon.

"I'm coming with you," Aemon demanded, holding onto her arm so she couldn't fly away without him.

"Very well then, let's go." Carabella grabbed him around the waist and made for the meadow.

Rogan swung his sword violently, as metal clashed upon metal. The other two guards slid down from their horses and stood by.

"Do you intend to fight all three of us?" The guard jested.

"If I must," Rogan replied, swinging his sword with all of his might.

"I'm getting a little bored of this," the guard yawned. Aggressively, he struck Rogan's sword with a mighty blow, driving Rogan to the ground. "I don't like taking the blood of a child, but you did ask for it, and you did kidnap the princess." He wielded his sword high over Rogan's head. Rogan could hear the princess scream as the sword started to come down upon him.

Suddenly, a multitude of fireballs whizzed over their heads. Rogan looked up to see his enemy struggling with his own sword.

"What kind of sorcery is this?" one of the guards called out, dodging the fireballs. The other guard tried to strike again, but his sword wouldn't budge. It was as if it was suspended in midair. Invisible, Aemon held the sword back while Carabella swirled around the other two.

"Spare him his life, I beg you, and I shall go back with you," the princess pleaded to the guards.

"Do as I say," the princess ordered. "Spare him his life and I shall come with you without a struggle."

"Very well, Princess Twila, we will spare his life," the guard reasoned. "Take the princess and leave him be." The guard took Rogan's sword from the ground and threw it as far as he could into the tall grass.

"It won't do you any good to retrieve it, since you don't know how to use it," he scoffed. One of the guards grabbed hold of the princess's arm, and roughly, pulled her up onto his horse. Twila looked down longingly at Rogan before they rode off.

"Princess," Rogan called out. Defeated, he fell to his knees and bowed his head.

"Boy, that was close," Aemon exclaimed.

"Too close," Carabella replied.

"How did you hold that sword back?" Rogan inquired.

"We can make ourselves invisible for a short amount of time," Aemon told him.

"All of you?"

"Most of the creatures who live in the enchanted forest," Carabella explained.

"So, what do we do now?" Aemon wondered.

"We come up with a different plan to save the princess, and the others," Rogan answered. He searched until he found his sword in the high grass. "We must hurry though, for time is against us."

The three made their way back to the enchanted forest. Carabella noticed that Rogan was limping. "You are hurt, young Rogan?" She seemed very concerned. Aemon looked over at her with a tinge of jealousy.

"No, just my pride," he told her. "If only I had my trusty horse with me, we would have surely made it over the meadow before Calabar's men had a chance to catch up to us. Heaven only knows what Alabash has done with him."

Aemon's pointy ears suddenly perked up. "What is it, Aemon?" Carabella wondered.

"I thought I heard something in the underbrush." They searched the area around them but they did not see anyone.

"It was probably just a meddlesome chipmunk," Carabella retorted. "You know how mischievous they can be." She turned her attention back to Rogan. "You must rest up, young Rogan, for the battle is not yet won. Aemon and I will come back later with food for you, and then together, we shall work on another plan to save the princess and the others."

Rogan leaned against the tree. He closed his eyes for just a few seconds, but he couldn't sleep. Images of the princess crowded his thoughts. "I will save you, Twila, I will, I promise," he called out.

"Not at the rate you're going, you won't," someone answered. "Who taught you how to fight anyway?"

"No one," Rogan replied, looking around for the source.

"Just as I thought. Rise to your feet, young one, and pick up your sword. Someone must teach you how to defend yourself. Hurry, there is no time to waste, for you have a princess to save."

Rogan held his sword out in front of him and listened as the voice instructed him on what to do. "Two hands together, that is your strength. Clasp them firmly," the voice called out as something struck the end of his sword. "Fight back boy, for I shall teach you how to use this sword properly for your own defense." Rogan listened intently to every word as his invisible partner swung his sword methodically. Feeling tired, he paused for a minute to catch his breath. "Whoever you are, why are you helping me?" Rogan wondered.

"Because I have seen you fight, and believe me, you need all the help that you can get," the voice told him. "Now, let us continue. I didn't make this sword for you for nothing." Rogan fought courageously as the instructor began to step up the challenge. Minutes turned into hours. A steady stream of sweat dripped down Rogan's face, but he didn't give up.

"I wonder how long you can remain invisible," Rogan inquired, moving about more aggressively.

"As long as I need to," the voice answered him.

"You know, I can see you," Rogan chuckled.

"Then you have earned my trust," the stocky troll replied. He laid his sword against a tree. "I almost forgot, you are human, you must be tired."

"Exhausted is more like it, but I'm ready for more." Rogan picked up his sword.

"What do we have here?" The troll picked up something shiny from the ground.

"That's my ruby," Rogan exclaimed. "It must have slipped out of my sock when we were fighting."

"Your sock? That's a funny place to keep it; and what are you doing with such a fine jewel?" the troll inquired.

"It was my mother's. It's all that I have left of her. I needed a more secure place to hide it in case I ever got robbed. I made a special pouch in one of my socks. Luckily Alabash's footmen didn't see it, or for sure, they would have taken it from me." The troll gave Rogan back his ruby. Rogan shined it up before putting it away.

"Come, let us sit and rest for a while," the troll offered. "There is one more skill that you need to learn, young Rogan. Finish the food that was left for you and then I will explain to you the art of fighting."

"Rogan was hungry. He finished his food quickly and then drank from the nearby spring. I'm ready to learn more," he told the troll.

"Good, now listen carefully, this skill, it deals not so much with the physical aspect of your being, but more with the mental. You need attitude, boy. You will need this in order to outwit your enemies. With attitude, they will learn to fear you."

"How do I go about getting this, attitude?" Rogan inquired.

"First, you must believe wholeheartedly in your convictions, then and only then, will you be able to draw your strength from within. If you believe that you can accomplish something worth accomplishing, then that inner strength will never fail you. You must learn to be confident in that which you do, and others shall look at you with great trepidation."

"It is true that newfound strength and attitude will come in handy to protect me from Calabar's men, but what I could really use right now is a pot of gold."

"A pot of gold, you say. How so?"

"As you know, a few nights back, I had in my possession a pouch full of golden nuggets. If I had not been robbed of my gold by the man named Alabash, I might have been able to barter with Calabar, not just for the sake of the people of my village, but for the princess's freedom, as well as that of her mother, and one other." Rogan looked very sad. "Now, Alabash stands to gain everything. If I cannot stop him, in less than forty-eight hours, the princess will be forced to marry someone she does not love, and my chance of rescuing anyone will be diminished. I swore that I shall do whatever I need to do to free them, or I will die trying," Rogan stated.

"Then rise to your feet, brave Rogan, for I have much more to teach you, and the night has fallen quickly upon us." The two sparred well into the early morning hours.

"You are a fast learner, brave Rogan, and I have taught you all that I know. It's time for you to sleep now, for you must be strong in both body and mind before your journey back. I shall leave you for the night. We will speak again tomorrow."

Rogan thanked his new friend for all that he had done for him. Quite exhausted, he lay his sword down by his side and curled up on the soft cushioned moss. "Attitude," he mumbled to himself, over, and over again, before falling asleep.

Rogan dreamed of the princess and the injustice of it all. His heart filled with rage when he thought of Calabar and Alabash and how in twenty-four hours the princess would be forced to marry an oath and a thief. When he woke, he took his sword in hand. With newly gained confidence, he sliced the sword through the air.

"Careful with that thing," a strange high-pitched voice rang out. A small green pointy-eared leprechaun suddenly appeared from out of nowhere.

Rogan rubbed his eyes in disbelief, as the tiny creature came toward him. "Was it not you who ordered the pot of gold?" he inquired. "You are Rogan, yes?"

"That is my name, but who are you?"

"I am Lare. My cousin, Travis Troll, sent for me. Luckily for you, I owed him a very big favor. He just called it in," Lare reluctantly replied. "I understand that you are in need of a pot of gold, on loan, of course." Lare raised both of his arms and sprinkled a handful of magic dust into the air. Suddenly, a black kettle filled to the rim with gold pieces appeared before Rogan. Rogan shielded his eyes from the glare. "So, tell me, what is it that you have planned with my pot of gold?"

Rogan filled Lare in quickly about the situation with the princess and the others. He told him all about Calabar and Alabash. Lare listened intently to his story, especially the part about Carabella's mother being held captive in Calabar's bed chamber.

"Approach the castle entrance, young Rogan, and present yourself to Calabar. Worry not, for the gold shall appear at your beckoning," Lare told him. "If you should get into any trouble, sprinkle some of this magic dust onto yourself and it will render you invisible, enough for you to make your escape. You will also need it to get through the meadow without being seen. Tell no one of our meeting or of my lending you my pot of gold or there could be consequences."

"It will be our secret," Rogan swore, "but, what if Calabar won't give back the gold?"

"Fear not, for soon after, it will turn into nothing but mere rocks," the tiny leprechaun chuckled. "Much luck to you on your journey lad."

Rogan made ready to go. When he got to the meadow, he sprinkled the magic dust over his body. Making it up to the large castle door without being noticed, Rogan knocked fiercely until the servant answered it.

"You again," the servant retorted, quite astonished to see him back. "Why the whole castle speaks your name." The servant looked behind him. "You have to be crazy to come back here? Leave now before the guards see you."

"I am not going anywhere," Rogan demanded, sticking his foot in the doorway, once again. "I must speak with Calabar, now!"

"Very well then," the servant mumbled, letting him in. Rogan entered the main dining hall where Calabar and Alabash sat together at a long table gorging on food and drink.

Calabar looked up from his meal with fury. "How dare you show your face here in my castle," he exclaimed, "especially after your failed attempt to kidnap my stepdaughter." Calibar rose from the table, spilling his glass of red wine all over the white linens Alabash had brought.

Alabash looked at the spoiled linens and then at Rogan. "My footmen will see to him," he replied angrily. "Seize him, and this time, make sure he does not escape."

Rogan quickly drew his sword, not allowing either of the guards to get anywhere near him. "Stay where you are," he told them both, "and I shall spare you."

"Perhaps he has come to help us celebrate my marriage to the princess," Alabash stated, slightly inebriated. "For in a few short hours, she shall be mine." He raised his wine glass in the air. "How I look forward to our wedding night," he boasted.

"I have come for no such celebration," Rogan replied heatedly. "As for you, Alabash, I am here to see that you will never claim the princess as your own."

"That is where you are wrong, young fool, for Alabash has already won the hand of the princess. He has brought me the finest of the riches of the land," Calabar stated.

"You mean the nuggets of gold that he stole from me," Rogan reminded him. "Tell me, were the rules of the contest meant for anyone, Calabar?"

"Yes, that was what I stated."

"Then do we still have until midnight?"

"That is correct," Calabar replied, "but we already know that you have nothing to offer. So clearly, Alabash is the victor."

"What if I could offer you fifty times as much as Alabash has stolen from me?"

"Then I would say that you are bluffing," Calabar retorted. "I've had enough of this nonsense. You two, handle this young fool quickly so that we may get on with our celebration."

Rogan struck the sword of one of the footmen with such force that it loosened his grip and sent the sword hurtling across the cold stone floor. The footman cowered, holding his hurt shoulder.

"Hear me out, Calabar; for I am offering you more riches than you have ever laid your eyes upon. I bring forth to you, not just a mere satchel of gold nuggets, but a Pot of Gold."

"A Pot of Gold?" Both Calabar and Alabash replied in sync. "So, tell me, where do you carry this pot of gold; in your sash?" Alabash jested.

"No, it's not in my sash." Rogan looked around and focused on the far side of the room. "It's right over there," he pointed. Calabar's eyes suddenly lit up as the sheen of the gold pieces lured him over to the deep black kettle. Looking somewhat like a mad man, he wasted no time inspecting the contents within. His hands slithered through the solid gold coins.

"You are pleased?" Rogan inquired. One could clearly see Calabar was elated.

"Then you agree that it is more than a mere satchel of nuggets?"

"Yes, much more," Calabar answered, mesmerized by the perfectly rounded coins.

"Do not let him fool you, Calabar, for surely they are fake," Alabash called out to him.

"I assure you; they are as real as the sun in the sky," Rogan stated. "Do tell, Calabar, who is the victor now?"

"With this pot of gold, you are," Calabar admitted, still drooling over the black kettle.

"You may have the most riches, but they will be of no use to you dead," Alabash shouted, again calling on his footmen. Rogan drew his sword as the sound of hard metal echoed across the empty hallway. He fought bravely, quickly bringing the one with the wounded shoulder to his knees. He drove the other one back to where he was cornered against the wall forcing him to drop his sword. He put his sword to the man's chest.

"Tell Calabar that you were the one who pierced my side and left me for dead," Rogan demanded.

"It is true," the footman muttered, "but it was not my intention to harm you. I was ordered by Alabash to do so. I gave you a flesh wound in order to trick him into thinking that I killed you."

"Why would you do such a thing?"

"Because I feared for my life," the footman told him.

"How is that?" Rogan inquired.

The footman bowed his head in shame. "I could not pay up on my taxes. I am indentured to Alabash and forced to serve him for the next three years. You must believe me; it is not a task that I would have volunteered to do."

"What is your name?" Rogan inquired.

"My name is Turin. I owned a farm a few hours west of here. Alabash was the town's mayor. Every year, he raised our taxes higher and higher. I tried in earnest to pay them, but I could not keep up. Alabash agreed to lower my debt so that I may keep my farm and so that my family would have a roof over their heads in exchange for three years of my servitude. For that, I am bound by contract to him and all of his evil doings," Turin spat out. "Do with me what you will, for in death, I shall be free of him and all of his trickery." Turin closed his eyes tightly.

"Open your eyes, Turin, for I shall not kill you, just as you did not kill me," Rogan reassured him. "I shall set you free on one condition."

"And what would that be?"

"That you do not, ever again, try to strike me with your sword."

"You have my word," Turin told him.

"Then as of this moment," Rogan stated, "you, Turin, are no longer bound in contract to this thief. You are free to go back to your family."

"Don't you listen to him, he has no say here," Alabash addressed Turin. "Pick up your sword and fight him, you fool."

"I shall no longer do your dirty work, Alabash." Turin stated bluntly.

"You, what are you waiting for," Alabash called out to his other footman. Reluctantly, the other man lunged forward, raising his sword high in the air.

Sala ran up the stone steps as quickly as she could to alert the young princess of what was happening. "Hurry," she panted, nearly out of breath. "Young Rogan is here in the castle, fighting for your freedom." The princess took to the stairs.

Rogan wielded his sword heroically as the other footman drove him back against the wall. Feeling a little weary, his legs began to weaken. "Attitude," an invisible voice called out to him.

"Attitude," Rogan mumbled, over and over again. He thought of the princess and the others all suffering at Calabar's hands. He thought of Alabash laying claim to the princess. His blood began to boil with rage. He could feel his strength suddenly come back to him. He sprang from the wall in a wild fury, wielding his sword aggressively at the already injured footman.

"This is an outrage," Calabar shouted. "Guards, guards," he called out. No one came. "Where are my soldiers?"

"You need not worry about them, young Rogan," a voice rang out. "They have been detained."

Rogan drove the footman across the room, ordering him to put down his sword.

"How is he doing, cousin?" An invisible voice inquired.

"Not too bad; he's holding his own. Don't you worry; I won't let anything happen to him. Besides, I'm not done with those two yet," the leprechaun stated, pointing over to Calabar and Alabash.

The princess shrieked with fear as she entered the room. Rogan quickly glanced her way, then drove the man back to the other side of the room. He lifted his sword high into the air to strike, but the footman suddenly seemed to trip over his own two feet, hitting his shoulder on Calabar's large oversized chair on the way down. An invisible Aemon stood over the fallen footman and smiled.

Turin took the sword from the other footman. "Brave Rogan, you could have been killed," the princess cried out. She ran swiftly into his arms. He lifted up her chin and gazed into her worried eyes. "I'm fine, Princess, and so shall you be." He then noticed that both Calabar and Alabash were nowhere in sight. "Where did they go?" he asked Turin.

"You'll never believe what I'm about to tell you, but I saw it with my very own eyes," Turin stated, a bit confused. "Both Calabar and Alabash were following the pot of gold. It was floating in the air as if the kettle grew wings." Turin shook his head. "Never before have I seen such witchery."

"I must go after them and bring them to justice," Rogan told Turin.

"I will go with you; I am in your debt now," Turin replied.

"No, I need you to stay here. You must protect the princess. There's no telling how many of Calabar's men will still be loyal to him. You can start by tying this one up," he told him, referring to the wounded footman. "I will take care of Calabar and Alabash myself," he replied.

"You go ahead, I will deal with this one. I vow that I will protect the princess with my life," Turin swore. "You have my word."

"I believe you. Take good care of her, for she is very special." Rogan turned to the princess and smiled. "When Turin is through here, you go with him to find your mother. Take Sala with you to tend to her needs," Rogan told her.

"Please be careful, brave Rogan," Twila called out to him.

"I shall, my princess."

"You will come back, won't you?" she wondered.

"I'll be back." He smiled, then slipped out into the crisp night air. Rogan could see the illuminating glare of the gold amid the meadow. "If only I had my horse," he sighed. "Surely I could catch up with them." Rogan heard some commotion in the distance. It sounded like the echo of a horse's hoof on the wooden bridge before him.

"Lightning, is that you?" he called out. Suddenly, Lightning bolted out of the darkness and brushed up against him. Rogan rubbed his head affectionately. "Hello, old friend, I never thought I'd see you again." He then noticed Carabella clinging to the horse's mane. "Carabella, it was you who brought my horse back to me, but how did you know where to find him?"

"That was easy; I asked the underworld and they led me right to him. Hurry Rogan, for Calabar and Alabash are heading towards the enchanted forest. I fear there could be trouble." Rogan quickly mounted his horse.

"Hold on tight, Carabella," he warned her, patting Lightning's side. "Fly like the wind, Lightning!" he shouted. The horse seemed to know just what to do.

What a sight it was as Lare led both beguiled men down the old forest road. He enticed them with spilled coins from the cauldron, in which the men greedily lined their pockets. Too weighty to walk any further, they fell to the forest floor.

Rogan hailed his horse just in time, as the ground began to shake violently, and the earth before him suddenly split in two. He and Carabella watched in silence, as long white milky arms reached up from below, pulling both Alabash and Calabar down with them. Both men shrieked with fear, but neither could move to save themselves, for their pockets of gold had become their anchors, securing them to the underworld forever.

Just as quickly as the earth opened up, it suddenly melded back together, leaving no trace of either man.

Lare grinned deviously, for he had changed the gold in their pockets to mere rocks. After securing his pot of gold, he turned and nodded to Rogan and Carabella before disappearing into thin air. Rogan grinned with satisfaction, turned his horse around, and headed back toward the castle.

When he returned, Turin was there waiting for him. "Turin, I thought you'd be long gone by now," Rogan inquired.

"I've waited this long to go home, a few more hours won't matter," Turin answered.

"So, how are things here?" Rogan asked, with much concern.

"Fear not, for all is well," Turin replied. "The princess, she rests by her mother's side."

"And what of the queen?"

"There is much good news to tell. The queen is very weak, but she is being well tended to. As for Calabar's soldiers, they were all grateful to be let go and they have returned back to their families."

"That is indeed good news," Rogan stated.

"And what of Calabar and Alabash?"

"They will not be a problem, ever again," Rogan told him. Just then, Sala walked into the room. She carried refreshments for the men.

"Brave Rogan, I am so glad that you have returned unharmed. Princess Twila will be relieved to know that you are well. I am to report to her immediately upon your return, for she will not sleep until I give notice of your well-being."

"Tell the princess and her mother to rest easily, for both Calabar and Alabash will never give either one of them reason to ever worry again," Rogan replied. "As for you Turin, you may leave as you wish. I'm sure your family anxiously awaits you."

"If it is all the same to you, I would like to remain here to offer my services to the queen," Turin offered. "I can send for my family. They will be safer here, now that both Alabash and Calabar are gone."

"I'm sure the queen will welcome you," Sala told him.

Rogan could feel Carabella stirring anxiously in his jacket pocket. "I have one more thing that I must do before I meet up with the princess, but I will be back soon." Rogan excused himself. He waited until he was out of sight of the two, then let Carabella out.

"Whew, it was getting a little stuffy in there," she retorted.

"Quickly Carabella, show me where Calabar's chamber is?"

"Follow me," she told him, then flew off. He followed her up the winding stone steps and down the dimly lit hallway to Calabar's chamber door. Rogan pushed the heavy door open.

"There in that chest. It has been locked since I was last here. Neither Aemon, nor I could get it open. I am worried, for I have not heard a whisper from my mother for some time now," Carabella sighed.

"Don't worry, Carabella, we will get the chest door open, and we will free your mother if I have to take it apart, piece by piece," Rogan told her. He grabbed the fireplace poker and wedged it into the locked chest door, pressing down on it with all of his might. The wood splintered and broke apart. Rogan pulled at the broken pieces, just enough to be able to get the glass cage out. He placed the cage by the window sill. Sadly, Adelina was lying lifelessly on the bottom of the cage floor.

"Oh no, we're too late," Carabella cried out.

"Step away," Rogan told her. He found a sharp object to crack the glass open from the opposite side of where Adelina lay. Sticking his hand through the hole he had made, he carefully picked up Adelina and brought her over to the bed. He laid her down gently on the soft woolen blanket. Carabella listened intently to her chest.

"She's breathing, but it is faint. We must get her some fresh air as soon as possible, brave Rogan." Rogan flung open the shutters, allowing the cool air to rush in.

"Breath mother, please, fill your lungs with the fresh crisp air," Carabella pleaded, watching for any signs of life. Adelina's chest rose up and down quickly. Her eyes suddenly began to flutter open.

"Carabella, my darling daughter; I feared that my end was near and that I would never see you again."

"I'm here, mother. You are free now. You must fight to survive."

Adelina looked anxiously around the room. "Calabar?"

Aemon suddenly came to their side. "Calabar has been sent to the underworld. You need not worry about him any longer," he told her. "I have seen it with my own two eyes."

"Then I am really free?"

"Yes, you are free," Carabella smiled. "We need to take her back to the enchanted forest, quickly," Carabella told Rogan. "We have special herbs there and medicines that will help make her well. The imps will know what to do for her. Medicine is their specialty."

"Then I shall take you back before I leave for my village," Rogan offered.

"That won't be necessary," Aemon interrupted. "I can take them. Briar Fox is waiting for us just outside the castle door."

"Then we must hurry," Rogan replied. He took the sash from his waist, wrapped Adelina in it, and then took to the stairs by leaps and bounds.

Aemon climbed on the back of Briar Fox. He reached his hand down for Adelina.

Somehow, he looked different to Carabella.

His hair was slicked back away from his face, and he wore a silk sash around his waist, much like young Rogan's. Carabella noticed a tiny wooden sword dangling at his side. "I will take Carabella and her mother back home," Aemon stated boldly. "The faster you ride to your village, young Rogan, the less time the princess will have to wait for your return."

"Yes, this is true," Rogan reasoned. "Very well then, I will leave them in your able hands, Sir Aemon." Carabella smiled approvingly, as she climbed up on Briar Fox.

"Much luck to you and your mother, Carabella," Rogan told her.

"And to you and the princess, brave Rogan." Carabella held her mother firmly in her arms, as the red fox turned to leave.

Days passed by without incident. Carabella tended to her mother high up in the tall pine tree.She sighed with relief as things seemed to be settling down in the forest, but the feeling of tranquility was short-lived as she watched the turbulence stirring down below.

"What's going on?" she called down to the imps.

"Gaelen has summoned us all to the pulpit."

"The pulpit, but there is no full moon tonight?"

"Gaelen did not give reason," they answered. "Hurry Carabella, for Nollan awaits us."

A cold wind suddenly whipped up from the north. Carabella couldn't help but shiver. It had been days since they returned, and so far, all had been well. "Surely," she reasoned, "Nollan would have called us all to the pulpit earlier if he knew what was truly going on." She heard Aemon calling for her from below. Carabella left her mother sleeping peacefully and flew down to meet him.

"I don't like this, Carabella," Aemon stated, nervously. "What if Nollan found out about Rogan, the princess, and your mother returning?"

"The imps and trolls promised not to say a word," Carabella told him.

"But do you trust them?"

"If they spoke, then I'm afraid that I shall be banished to the Underworld, forever," Carabella quivered, hanging her head down, despondently. She could see the look of fear in Aemon's eyes. "Don't worry Aemon, it'll be okay. They can't all be that bad, after all, they did help us out."

Aemon took her hand in his. "I will stand with you, Carabella." Slowly, they made their way through the forest. The crowd gathered around as Gaelen began to count heads. He glanced over, uneasily, at Carabella. "This meeting shall come to order," he called out, just as Nollan made his way to the pulpit. There wasn't a sound, not even the rustling of the leaves underfoot as Nollan stared out into the trembling crowd. His large gray eyes focused solely on Carabella. She looked guiltily toward the ground.

"Carabella Snow, step forward," Nollan summoned. Carabella swallowed hard. All eyes were upon her. With buckled knees, she took a step forward. "Come closer," Nollan ordered. Carabella stopped within two feet of the pulpit. Nollan spoke firmly.

"Carabella, it has come to my attention that you have broken not just one, but many of the rules of the enchanted forest. What say you, child?"

"I, I…" Carabella tried to speak but the words wouldn't come out.

"Do you deny these allegations?" Nollan asked her.

"I cannot," she quivered. Sighing loudly, Nollan looked dismayed. "What am I to do with you, Carabella? You do know the punishment for breaking the rules, don't you?"

"Yes," she managed to blurt out.

"You know that I cannot let such deception go without punishment, for if everyone did as they pleased in this forest, we would all live a life of chaos. Do you have anything to say on your behalf, young lady?"

"I'm afraid not," she gulped.

"Then you don't deny any wrongdoing?" he asked.

"I deny nothing," Carabella stated, with a newfound courage. "Be it as it is, I shall take my punishment justly."

"Very well then," Nollan answered, "Carabella Snow, because you have blatantly gone against the rules of the enchanted forest, and because you have inadvertently put our people at risk, time and time again, I hereby banish you to…"

"Wait," a voice suddenly rang out from the woods. A look of shock came over the crowd as Adelina Snow pushed her way through the crowd.

"Adelina!" Nollan exclaimed.

"Yes, it is I." Adelina stood stoically beside her daughter.

"Mother, you are not well, you must go back and rest," Carabella commented.

"I will be fine, Carabella. I will not let them banish you to the underworld, not when it was my fault that you broke the rules. Hear me Nollan, for there are things that I need to say on my daughter's behalf."

Nollan hesitated for a moment. "Very well, you may speak."

"Yes, it is true that Carabella crossed the boundaries of the enchanted forest, but it was not her fault that she did, it was mine. If I had not called out to her from within my glass prison, she would not have come in search of me."

"Your glass prison?" Nollan inquired.

"Yes, that is where I have been for the past few years; imprisoned in the castle by the man who called himself Calabar. If it had not been for Carabella and the young man they call Rogan, I would not be alive right now."

"Welcome back, Adelina," some of the braver voices called out to her.

"Silence," Nollan shouted, raising his cane over his head. "This is not a time for celebration. What we have here is a serious situation. Do you not realize that the fate of your very own lives has now been jeopardized? How many others know about us here in the forest?"

"Calabar was the only one who knew about the fairies," Carabella noted. "Now that he is gone, there is no more threat to any of us."

"What of this young man, Rogan? Did you not keep him hidden in the forest?" Nollan blurted out. "Did you not think that I would find out?"

"I do not deny helping him," Carabella answered truthfully. "I did not ask for him to come, nor did I seek him out. He was injured, left there for dead. I merely helped him to recover his wounds. If helping another creature warrants punishment, then I am guilty, and I will accept my just dues, but only under one condition."

Nollan's nostrils flared. "You are in no position to ask for anything, Carabella."

"I beg that you listen to my pleas, oh Mighty Nollan. Banish me to the Underworld, if that is your will, but let my mother live here freely among her peers, for she has already suffered a lifetime at the hands of Calabar."

"And you would take your punishment without any further discourse?" Nollan asked.

"Yes, you have my word," Carabella answered remorsefully.

"Very well then, I shall meet your condition. I shall allow your mother to live freely here among her friends and family," Nollan agreed. "I am sorry that it has to come to this, Carabella, but I cannot allow this disobedience to go unpunished. I have no choice but to banish you to the Underworld." Carabella remained silent as the crowd mumbled with disapproval.

Aemon took a step forward. "If you banish Carabella, then you must banish me too, for I was the one who found young Rogan by the side of the road."

"Do not listen to him," Carabella bellowed. "He had nothing to do with this."

"Not only did I tend to his wounds here in the forest, but I have also been to the castle and back."

"Is this true, Aemon?" Nollan inquired.

"Don't listen to him. He's just making it all up," Carabella stated.

"I stand by what I say. If you banish Carabella, then you must banish me too."

"And me too," Aemon's little brother Filo suddenly came forward.

"And what hand did you have in all of this, young Filo?"

"I asked for the help of my friend, the fox, so that my big brother could ride to the castle and bring Carabella and her mother back."

"And I made a nice soft bed for Carabella's mother, high up in the pine tree, so she could rest comfortably," one of the fairies admitted.

"I too tended to Adelina and young Rogan with special herbs and potions," another fairy confessed.

"We were the ones who gave the fairies the potions to help Adelina and young Rogan get well," the imps admitted.

"It was I who brought tea for young Rogan when he was lying ill in the forest," Lily Frost spoke out.

"I was the one who brewed the tea for Lily Frost to give to young Rogan," Petunia Petal noted. Nollan looked over the crowd, dumbfounded.

"I changed the herbs on the young boy's wounds so he would heal quicker," another of the fairies soon confessed. Soon after, others started to come forward. "I left water for him in a leather satchel," one of the imps admitted.

"I gathered berries and fruit for young Rogan to eat," Dana Dew Drop confessed.

"It was I who taught him how to fight," Travis the troll stated, boldly.

"You Travis, my most trusted troll? Why you have never kept a secret in your life."

"The boy needed help," Travis replied earnestly.

"I had my hand in it too," Timkin added.

"You, Timkin, protector of the old forest road?" Nollan asked, in disbelief.

"I turned my head when the others came close to the forbidden forest road, and I helped Travis summon his cousin Lare, who lent the boy his pot of gold," Timkin confessed.

"A Pot of Gold, was it?" Nollan replied, scratching his chin feverishly.

"Yes, he needed to borrow it in order to save the princess, and her mother, the queen," Timkin clarified.

"Not to mention our very own Adelina," another voice called out from the crowd.

"The princess?" Nollan inquired, unaware of her involvement. "This just gets better and better." Nollan looked over at his very own family. "What of you gnomes?"

"I gave Travis the finest steel I had so he could make a sword for the boy and teach him how to defend himself," Nollan's own brother, Eton, declared.

"I see," Nollan replied, astonished by what he was witnessing. "Is there anyone here in this forest that did not have a hand in helping this young man?" Not one hand went up. "What of you, Gaelen?"

"Guilty," Gaelen replied, in a high squeaky voice. "I merely listened to his prayers. He was very sincere, Nollan. He prayed for us all so that we would stay safe and protected here in the forest. He called us his friends. Anyway, I made him sign a waiver. Here, see for yourself."

Gaelen took a small scroll from his vest pocket and started to unroll it. "Young Rogan swore that he would never discuss the creatures of the enchanted forest, not with anyone. It's signed in his own blood. You know what that means, Nollan." Gaelen pointed to the dried-out signature. "Look at the fine print, there are consequences if he disobeys, and he's agreed to them all." He handed the scroll over to Nollan. Nollan grumbled as he read the agreement.

"Still, the question remains, what shall I do with the lot of you? Rules have been broken and those who broke them need to be punished; but if I banished you all here today to the Underworld, there would be no one left in the forest to carry on with the chores." Nollan sat down on a nearby stump and thought deeply about the situation. Every little creature around him remained silent, waiting anxiously for his decision.

"Are you forgetting something, Nollan," Gaelen whispered over to him. "Wasn't it you who ordered the grounds to open up and swallow both Alabash and Calabar? Does that not make you a part of all of this?"

"Did not Calabar have it coming for what he did to poor Adelina?" One of the imps spat out, trying to rile the crowd.

"Silence," Nollan shouted, a bit embarrassed, knowing that he was just as guilty as the rest of them. Nollan pondered, as the crowd waited for his judgment. A slight grin suddenly overcame him, and a feeling of pride began to fill his heart. He had witnessed something here today that he had never seen before in all his life as ruler of the little people. All of the creatures of the forest had come together, not only to help out a young injured boy, but bravely came forward in an effort to save one of their own from eternal banishment. Nollan looked down at Carabella forgivingly. "Tell me, Carabella, do you foresee any other pressing matters that will again call you away from the forest?"

"None, Sir," Carabella replied, diligently. "I am content right here where I belong, now that my mother is home."

"Then consider this a warning to all, for I will not be so tolerant the next time around," Nollan cautioned. "Carabella, and the rest of you, your punishment is as follows; for the next three months, each one of you shall work extra long hours tending to the flora and fauna of the forest. I want every leaf on every tree polished until it shines, every broken branch mended, and every bird in the nest made more comfortable. The streams shall be cleared of any debris and the pulpit area swept clean daily." Nollan put his hands on his hips. "Well, what are you all waiting for? You have work to do." He chuckled under his breath as the crowd began to scatter in all directions. "Not you, Adelina, you and I have much to catch up on."

It was a long week, as Twila waited anxiously for Rogan's return from his village. It was early in the morning when he finally got back, just in time for fresh bread right out of the oven. Sala was very happy to see him. She smeared plenty of jam on his roll and filled him in on everything that was happening at the castle. Sala sent the maidens up to awaken the princess to let her know that Rogan was back.

Rogan was just finishing up the last of the roll when Twila came running in. She was still in her nightgown and barefooted. "Rogan," she called out to him. It was no doubt that she would have put her arms around him if Sala hadn't been in the room.

Rogan's eye lit up with delight. "It's nice to see you again, Princess."

"It's nice to see you too. Tell me, how did everything go with the villagers?"

"They were very happy to have the queen's protection. They asked if you could thank her for them?"

"You can thank her yourself," Twila exclaimed. "As a matter of fact, she's waiting to meet you. Let me go and see if she is up."

"You might want to change out of your night clothes while you're up there," Sala chuckled.

"Yes, yes of course." Twila turned to Rogan. "Will you excuse me?"

Rogan smiled at her. "I'll be right here waiting, Princess." She smiled back.

"I shan't be long."

Rogan tucked in his shirt, frantically tried to slick back his straight long hair in the reflection of a pan. Sala could tell that he was uneasy.

"You look fine, young Rogan. I am sure that the queen will love you. The princess has spoken most highly of you. In the meantime, would you like another buttered roll?"

"No, thank you," Rogan replied anxiously. "I am a little nervous. What do I say to a queen? Do I bow when I see her? Do I take her hand?"

Sala smiled. "Just be yourself, Rogan, and all will fall into place." One of the queen's personal hand maidens came down to fetch him. "The queen is ready for you now," she told Rogan. Rogan stood frozen. He looked over at Sala.

"Go ahead, don't keep the queen waiting," she told him. Rogan took a deep breath, then followed the maiden into the hallway. She led him up to the queen's chambers. Rogan entered the room slowly. Princess Twila rose to greet him.

"Welcome, Brave Rogan," the princess addressed him.

"It is good to see you again, Princess." Rogan smiled fondly.

"Mother, this is the man who rescued us," Twila exclaimed.

The queen was sitting up on the bed. She was still too weak to get up. "Come closer, young Rogan, so that I can see you better by the morning's light." Rogan did as she asked. The queen looked up at him and smiled. "I cannot begin to thank you enough for your courage and your bravery."

"I was happy to help the princess," Rogan told her.

"It's a miracle how you, nearly a man, not only outsmarted Calabar, but that mongrel, Alabash, as well."

"Believe me, my Queen, I had a lot of help," Rogan replied. He glanced over at Twila, for both had sworn their oath of never telling anyone about the creatures that lived in the enchanted forest, not even to the queen.

"I am gratefully indebted to you, young man, and I wish to pay you back for saving, not only my life but that of my precious daughter. Tell me, what is it that you desire?"

"You already gave me your promise to protect the people of my village. For that, they asked me to thank you. I speak to you as a man, asking for nothing more than peace and harmony for them, and everyone else throughout the valley. No longer do we have to worry about Calabar's army threatening our very existence. That is all I asked for."

"Are you sure that is all?" The queen looked from Rogan to Twila. Rogan wasn't exactly sure what she meant. The queen could see that he needed a little push. "Tell me, Rogan, will you be returning back to your village for good?"

"I'm not sure," he answered.

"I feel that there is one other important matter that needs to be addressed," the queen stated. "I have been informed about a certain contest of the sorts, and although initiated by Calabar himself, I feel compelled to honor the agreement which was made." The queen could tell that neither Rogan nor her daughter had the courage to say what they really felt about each other, so she decided to be straightforward. "Tell me, Rogan, is this your satchel of gold?"

"It is my village's gold, not mine alone. I brought it here to barter with Calabar."

"No one else has come forward with anything more, and since the deadline has passed, that makes you the rightful victor of this contest," the queen stated. "Young Rogan, answer me truthfully, do you wish for the hand of my daughter in marriage?"

Rogan swallowed hard. He took some time to find his voice.

"I would like that very much, but I am not worthy of the princess's love."

"And why would you think that?" the queen inquired.

"Before I came here to the castle, I herded sheep, and when someone needed a new roof, I mended it. When a villager needed carpentry work, I fixed things, and when my village needed defending, I defended it. I cannot give the princess the life that she expects. I have nothing to offer her," Rogan replied sadly.

"Your village must think very highly of you, entrusting you with their gold. It was you that they chose to bring it forward to represent your village, did they not? That says much about you," the queen noted.

"It is only because I was familiar with this part of the land. You see, once, a long time ago, my parents lived not far from here. I didn't remember before, but when the princess and I were on the run from the soldiers, I seemed to know my way through the old trail behind the castle," Rogan stated. "I remember now, my father used to take me to the stream back there where we swam and we fished. I was just a child."

"And where are your parents now?" the queen asked.

"They were killed."

"Oh, I'm very sorry. May I ask how it happened?"

"My father came home late one night and woke us from our sleep. He told my mother and I that we had to leave immediately. We were to take only the clothes on our backs and a few other small items. He said that we must hurry. He packed up our horses and off we went into the cold night. We rode for days before we stopped to rest. The horses were tired, and we were weary," Rogan continued. "Little did I know that it would be my parent's last night alive."

"What happened, Rogan," Twila inquired.

"It was late. I was down by the water with my father's horse when I heard some commotion. I crawled up the river bank and saw movement. It was soldiers. There were three of them. They had ambushed my parents as they sat by the fire, then took the other two horses, and left as quickly as they came. When I saw my parents lying there, lifeless, on the ground, I was in shock. I gathered up what I could, climbed up on my father's horse, and followed the river," Rogan went on. "Fearing that those men might come back for me, I rode until I could ride no more. I ended up cold and hungry, lying in a ditch by the side of the road near the village that I have just come from. Kind people took me in and saw to Lightning, my father's horse."

"Lightning?" the queen exclaimed.

"Yes, my horse. He's the only thing that I have left of my father."

The queen sat up, sternly. "Tell me, young Rogan, what was your father's name?"

"Edward, his name was Edward."

"And your mother?"

"Judith." The queen gasped, then fell back onto the pillow.

"Mother are you alright?" Twila asked, concerned.

"Do you remember, if your mother had something on her, something that might be worth some money?"

"She did," Rogan commented. He dug into his pocket. "This was clutched in her hand when I found her." He showed them the ruby.

"May I?" the queen asked. Rogan handed it to her. Tears began to flow down her cheeks.

"Mother, what is it?" Twila put her arm around her.

"I knew your parents very well, young Rogan. Your father was a very brave man. He was our head knight, in charge of all of our soldiers. He helped to keep peace and order throughout our land. My husband looked on him like a son," the queen went on. "Long after my husband died, Calabar came into my life. I know now that it was Calibar's henchmen that not only killed your parents but probably my husband, as well. Calabar did all that he could do to charm me, but I would not fall for his trickery. I told him to leave. That is when he took my daughter from me, and he told me that the only way that I would get her back, alive, was if I married him. I had no choice on the matter. I fought him hard, but he brought in his own army of cutthroats and kept my darling girl from me. We had little freedom, and little say," the queen continued. "Your father was very loyal to me. Those who remained loyal were killed by Calabar's men. It was I who sent your father and your mother away. Your mother was my most trusted confidante. I gave her this ruby so that they would have enough money to go far away, but your father, he told me that he would use the money to build up an army. He promised to come back with a new army and take down Calabar. Now I know why he never came back," the queen sighed.

"I didn't know any of this," Rogan replied.

"How could you, you were just a child. You were lucky to have escaped with your life," the queen reasoned. "In a way though, your father, he did keep his promise. All these years later, you, his son, came along, and you, almost single-handedly, exacted that very revenge that I dreamed of for so many years." "Brave Rogan, if you think that you are not worthy of my daughter's hand in marriage, you are very wrong, for you are exactly the man that I had wished for my daughter to one day marry. So, I ask you, be truthful, do you have any feelings for Twila?"

"From the moment that I laid my eyes upon her, my heart has pounded wildly from within, and with every step that I am away from her, I long to be with her even more," Rogan answered.

The queen interrupted. "Then, you do wish to marry her?" Rogan turned to Twila. "If she will have me?"

The queen then addressed her daughter. "And what of you, Twila?"

"I wish to be with this man, not because of the gold that he has brought forth, but because I find him the kindest, bravest, most courageous man that I have ever met," Twila replied. "It does not matter to me whether you are Rogan, the sheepherder, or Rogan, son of Edward, Protector of Castle Cragg. I would be honored to spend the rest of my life by your side."

The queen took her daughter's trembling hand and placed it into Rogan's. "Then it is settled. Sir Rogan, bravest in the land, I give to you the hand of my daughter."

Sala and the two handmaidens were in the hallway listening intently to every word, trying to hold back their sobs. The queen shook her head and smiled. "You ladies may come in." The three joined in, elated about the news. "Ladies, we are going to have a great big feast to celebrate, not only for the giving of these two in marriage, but I must address the people of the kingdom and tell them that things will be better, for all, from here on end. Now ladies, go and spread the word, come next Sunday, all are invited."

"Next Sunday, gosh that doesn't give us much time," Sala deducted. "Ladies, come, we have a lot to do. There's food to be prepared, dishes to gather, silverware to be polished, people to invite, and so much more," Sala exclaimed. "Let us go and get started." The ladies hurried out the door.

"Brave Rogan, along with marriage comes responsibility. I do believe that you have earned the right to oversee my new army. You will take your father's place as my head soldier and help me keep peace and prosperity in the land for generations to come. You may gather your villagers together and bring them back here, for I shall guarantee that every family receives a fertile piece of land so they may farm and grow more than enough food to feed their families. To show them my good faith, you may take this satchel of gold back to your village and use it for expenses for their journey here. Bring Turin with you and when you return, we will have our wedding. Now you two, go and find some quiet place where you can talk. I'm sure you have much to discuss."

Rogan and the princess tried to find a private place to talk, but Sala already had the household in a frenzy, as they prepped for the feast.

"Come with me," Rogan told her. He took her hand and led her into a corner by the fire. "Come closer." He took the magic dust the leprechaun had given him earlier and sprinkled it over the two of them.

"What is this," Twila inquired.

"Magic dust. I only have a little left, but it should do the job. It will render us invisible for just a short time. I used it to get through the meadow and past the guards." Rogan pulled Twila close and kissed her passionately. "I'm sorry," he told her, "I just wanted to kiss you for so long now." The princess smiled at him and kissed him back. "Me too," she whispered.

"You will come back soon from your village, won't you?"

"Lightning and I will fly like the wind, and return even before you have a chance to miss me."

"But I miss you already, and you haven't even gone yet," the princess told him. "I know I seem foolish, but I have never felt this way about anyone before."

"Me neither," Rogan replied.

The creatures of the enchanted forest remained invisible as Rogan rode through the old forest road with his entourage. He knew well enough to keep going, but it didn't stop him from tossing a small piece of paper, bearing Carabella's name, onto the ground.

Rogan looked back proudly at the cascade of villagers who followed him faithfully, knowing that up ahead, there were only good things waiting for them.

Carabella and Aemon sat, hand in hand, in the tall stately pine tree, listening to the church bells ringing throughout the meadow. Carabella knew that it was the day that Sir Rogan would marry his princess bride.

"Oh, how I wish we could all be there to see it," she exclaimed.

"Bite your tongue, Carabella," Aemon replied. "Haven't we gotten into enough trouble already?"

"It was just a thought, Aemon. Don't worry, I wasn't planning on any more excursions. I can still be happy for the princess though, can't I? She now has her own brave knight, as I have mine." Carabella kissed Aemon's cheek affectionately. The tips of his pointy ears suddenly turned a bright shade of red.

"Are you ever going to tell me what the note said that Rogan left for you?" A jealous Aemon inquired.

"Young Rogan told me that on this date when day turns to night, he will have his trumpeters call out three times to let me know that all is well with the people of the kingdom. In return, I should send him up a fireball, but only if all is well with us here in the forest."

"That was nice of him to be so concerned, but from now on, Carabella Snow, I will be the one making sure that all is well with you."

"Agreed," Carabella replied. She smiled proudly as she looked admiringly at her own little hero.

Sure to his word, the sound of trumpets blared three times during the night. Carabella stood high on a tree branch gathering up as many electric currents as she could carry in her tiny hands.

Aemon looked toward the sky, as Carabella hurled the biggest fireball that she had ever made high up into the air. The other fairies all joined in. The young Prince watched from the balcony as the fireball's suddenly exploded and lit up the sky. He was relieved for Carabella and the others, for he knew that all was well within the enchanted forest. Rogan glanced at his beautiful wife and smiled. Never had he been happier.

The night was still as the wind fell silent. There was neither a whisper nor a murmur to be heard. Aemon slept peacefully by Carabella's side. As for Carabella, she tossed and turned. Too restless to sleep, she dreamed of adventures yet to come.

May your life be as wondrous and as magical as the creatures of the Enchanted Forest!

CPSIA information can be obtained
at www.ICGtesting.com
Printed in the USA
JSHW011451190522
26064JS00002B/8